MY LiFE

BOOKS BY BILL MYERS

Children's Series

McGee and Me! (12 books)

The Incredible Worlds of Wally McDoogle:
—My Life As a Smashed Burrito with Extra Hot Sauce
—My Life As Alien Monster Bait
—My Life As a Broken Bungee Cord
—My Life As Crocodile Junk Food
—My Life As Dinosaur Dental Floss
—My Life As a Torpedo Test Target
—My Life As a Human Hockey Puck
—My Life As an Afterthought Astronaut
—My Life As Reindeer Road Kill
—My Life As a Toasted Time Traveler
—My Life As Polluted Pond Scum
—My Life As a Bigfoot Breath Mint

Fantasy Series

Journeys to Fayrah:
—The Portal
—The Experiment
—The Whirlwind
—The Tablet

Teen Series

Forbidden Doors:
—The Society
—The Deceived
—The Spell
—The Haunting
—The Guardian
—The Encounter

Adult Books

Christ B.C.
Blood of Heaven
Threshold

the incredible worlds of Wally McDoogle

MY LIFE as a BIGFOOT BREATH MINT

BILL MYERS

Thomas Nelson, Inc.
Nashville • London • Vancouver

MY LIFE AS A BIGFOOT BREATH MINT

Managing Editor: Laura Minchew
Project Editor: Beverly Phillips

Library of Congress Cataloging-in-Publication Data

Myers, Bill, 1953–
My life as a bigfoot breath mint / Bill Myers.
p. cm. — (The incredible worlds of Wally McDoogle ; bk. #12)
Summary: Wally's visit to the Fantasmo World amusement park, where his Uncle Max works as a stuntman, turns into a disaster involving computer errors, runaway rides, and other outrageous mistakes.
ISBN 0–8499–3876–7 (pbk.)
[1. Amusement parks—Fiction. 2. Stunt performers—Fiction. 3. Uncles—Fiction. 4. Christian life—Fiction. 5. Humorous stories.] I. Title. II. Series: Myers, Bill, 1953–
Incredible worlds of Wally McDoogle ; #12.
PZ7.M98234Myd 1997
[Fic]—dc20 96–32349
CIP
AC

Printed in the United States of America

97 98 99 00 QBC 9 8 7 6 5 4

For Roberta Sanford—
who taught me how to "read."

"Honor your father and your mother.
Then you will live a long time. . . ."

—Exodus 20:12

Contents

Chapter 1

Just for Starters . . .

"Jump!" my little sister Carrie screamed, "Jump, Wally, jump!"

"I can't. My shoelace is stuck!"

"Then unstick it," Mom shouted.

"If I could unstick it, I wouldn't be stuck!"

Ah yes, welcome to another not-so-minor McDoogle mishap. . . .

Just a few seconds earlier I'd been playing tug-of-war with one of Mom's suitcases. I had been trying to pull it off the luggage carousel at the airport. And it had been trying to pull me on.

Unfortunately, it won.

It's not that I'm a wimp or anything. It's just that my older twin brothers, Burt and Brock, got all the muscle DNA in the family. But that's okay; there's more to being a seventh-grade guy than just having muscles. There's . . . there's . . .

well okay, maybe there isn't. At least not when you're battling with your mom's overstuffed luggage.

Of course I had tried to jump off the luggage carousel. But as I've so carefully pointed out, my shoelace was caught and—

"Wally, look out!"

I glanced up. Directly above me a gazillion suitcases tumbled out of the overhead chute. They bounced down the ramp heading directly toward . . . you guessed it, the one and only me.

Great, I sighed, *just great. I finally get to go to California, and I don't even get out of the airport before I become Samsonite road kill.*

But, being the inventive type of genius I am, I turned to my family and quite calmly screamed my head off.

"SOMEBODY HELP ME!"

My brothers were the first to ignore my request. It's not that they're insensitive or anything. I'm sure they wanted to help. It's just hard to help someone when you're falling on the floor laughing.

But not Mom. No sir. With the courage and dedication only a mother can have for her child, she turned to Dad and said, "So Herb, shouldn't you be doing something?"

To which Dad heroically muttered, "I suppose." (I sometimes get the feeling that Dad would love me more if I had followed in Bert's and Brock's footsteps as All-School Superjocks. Instead I'm the All-School Punching Bag.)

By now everyone in Baggage Claim was staring. If my best friend Wall Street had been around, she'd have charged admission. It looked like I was performing this one for my favorite charity . . . The Society for the Prevention of Cruelty to Dork-oids.

But not to worry, good old Dad had promised Mom that he'd save me. And if there is one thing he's learned over the years, it's not to disappoint good old Mom.

Anyway, he heroically leaped to my rescue.

Unfortunately, his leaper isn't as heroic as it used to be. Actually, the leaping was okay. But the landing part got kind of messy.

"Oww!" he cried as he landed beside me. "My back! My back!"

Normally I would have offered him words of sympathy. But since those suitcases kept tumbling toward us, and since he wouldn't have back pain in heaven, I figured why bother.

And then, just when we were about to be smashed flatter than today's special at the House of Pancakes, an incredible bronzed form leaped over us.

With superhero strength, he threw his body between us and the falling suitcases.

BAM, THUD, SPLAT!

He took the full impact of the luggage as it smashed into his megastrong body.

The crowd gasped in admiration.

But he wasn't done. Not yet. Next he ripped off his leather jacket and stuffed it between the conveyor belts. The luggage carousel began to growl and shudder. Then it began to shake, rattle, and roll. Finally the whole machine ground to a stop.

I was speechless. It was the most heroic rescue I had ever seen. The people around us started to clap and cheer.

And the superhunk? After taking a couple of bows, he dropped to my side. With an incredible smile, he said, "Hi, you must be Wally McDoogle."

My mouth dropped open. Had my reputation for klutz-oidness spread all the way to the West Coast?

"Well, yeah," I stuttered. "But how did, who are—"

"I'm your Uncle Max. I haven't seen you since you were a couple of years old," he said, brushing his thick blond hair out of his deep blue eyes.

"You're . . . you're my dad's brother?" I stuttered.

"That's right, kiddo. Welcome to L.A."

* * * * *

Now, I'd heard stories about Uncle Max all of my life. He was the rebel of the family. While Dad is more the go-to-church-and-try-to-do-the-right-thing kind of guy, Uncle Max is more of the if-it-feels-good-do-it-and-keep-on-doing-it-until-you-drop-dead-from-doing-it-too-much variety. That may be part of the reason he is one of the top-paid stunt men in Hollywood. In fact, he is so good that he has his very own stunt show at the world-famous movie theme park, Fantasmo World.

We'd bugged Dad for years about going to Los Angeles, where he'd grown up, and visiting his brother. But he'd always found an excuse. It took some distant great aunt's death to finally bring us out. It seems Great Aunt Thelma had made Dad the executor of her will (that's the guy in charge of dividing up all the loot), so he had to come out. And since there was no way he could do so without bringing us (oh, he could try, but he wouldn't live to tell about it), here we were.

And there, towering above me in all of his coolness, was Uncle Max.

The first thing you notice are his ultracool looks: great tan, huge muscles, and thick blond hair. In fact, as we headed to his car with our bags, I bet there wasn't a single babe who didn't check him out.

And he checked them out right back.

Cool.

Then there was his even cooler sports car. Granted, it was a little crowded with all seven of us (not to mention our luggage) crammed in. But I gotta tell you, once we got going, that puppy could scoot.

"Man't mou mo mower?!"

"What's that, Herb?" Uncle Max called to the backseat.

It was a little difficult for Dad to speak since one of Carrie's suitcases had jammed against his mouth, but he tried again. *"Man't mou mo mower?!"*

Mom translated. "He's wondering if you can't go slower."

Uncle Max laughed. "Don't be such an old lady, Herbie. This little baby doesn't really get going until it hits ninety." He glanced into the mirror. "Uh-oh, it looks like we've got company."

"Huh?" Dad asked.

Uncle Max hit the gas as he shouted, "Hang on!"

We shot forward. The acceleration shoved us so deep into our seats that for a moment I thought I'd landed in the trunk. He started zipping in and out of lanes like some skier in the Winter Olympics. And with each swerve and turn, our suitcases and ourselves flew back and forth inside the car.

SCREECH . . .

"WAAAAY!"

SQUEAL . . .

"WOOOAH!"

SKIIID . . .

"WAUGHHH!"

Everyone was shouting and having a great time.

Everyone but Dad. He was shouting, too, though I think he missed the "great time" part.

"Hang on," Uncle Max yelled. "A couple of thugs

have been following us since the airport. It's time to give them the slip."

While Dad was busy having cardiac arrest, the rest of us were having the ride of our lives. Think of it. We'd barely been in California an hour, and we were already in the middle of a car chase right out of the movies. But this was no movie. This was better than a movie. This was reality!

Unfortunately, reality didn't last nearly long enough. Just when we were really getting into it, Uncle Max dropped back down to his cruising speed of 90 miles per hour.

What a disappointment for us.

What a relief for Mom and Dad.

And since the luggage had shifted (my sister's suitcase was now embedded in my left armpit), my father was finally able to shout, "What do you think you're doing?!"

Uncle Max smiled. "Relax Herbie. It's just a couple of fellows interested in collecting on some gambling debts."

"Yeah, but—"

"I've been giving them the slip for weeks. No biggie."

"Yeah, but—"

"Listen," he said, suddenly changing subjects, "I've gotta be on the set at six tonight. We're doing a big stunt at the Santa Monica Pier for the new Arnold Swizzlenoggin picture."

"You know Arnold Swizzlenoggin!" we all chimed in at the same time. (Well, not all of us—Dad was still working on his, "Yeah, buts.")

"Know him?" Uncle Max laughed. "I've been his stunt double for years."

"You're Arnold Swizzlenoggin's stunt double?" I asked.

"Oh yeah. Any time there's a stunt that he's afraid to do, he calls me in." Suddenly his eyes lit up. "Hey, I've got a great idea. Why don't you come down to the pier and watch?"

"Cool!" we cried.

"What about your show at Fantasmo World?" Dad asked.

"That's my day job. You can see that tomorrow. I do these other stunts to pick up pocket change. You know, a few thousand here, a few thousand there. So what do you say, Herbie?"

"Can we, Dad?" we all begged.

"Well, it's been a long flight, I don't—"

"Should be fun," Uncle Max interrupted. "And since we don't have to be there for a couple of hours—"

"Well, I—"

"That'll give you time to unpack, rest a little, and—"

"Well, I—"

"I'll tell Mercedes, the cook, to fix you up a nice—"

"You have a cook?" Mom asked, sounding impressed.

"Oh yeah. Just say the word, and she'll fix you a nice dinner to go. Then you can all come down and watch me work."

"All right!" we shouted.

Max chuckled. "That is, if it's cool with the ol' stick-in-the-mud back there."

"Can we, Dad?"

Dad swallowed hard. I could tell he was feeling the pressure—which was exactly why we were staring at him.

"Well, I—"

Great! He was back to his "Well, I's" again. We had him on the ropes.

"What say, Herb?" Max grinned at him.

"Well, I—"

"Time to show your little family what their Uncle Max can really do?"

We continued to look at Dad.

Poor guy. He didn't have a chance. Each of us kids gave him our best puppy dog stare. You know, the one where you look all sweet and innocent?

He cleared his throat.

We stared harder.

"Well . . ." he coughed slightly. "Sure, why not?"

We all cheered.

But we wouldn't have cheered if we'd known what was coming up.

Chapter 2

Action!

If Uncle Max's car was cool, his home was even cooler. He had a giant house that overlooked the Pacific Ocean, a huge swimming pool complete with a waterfall, and for Burt and Brock's amusement, the kitchen had a refrigerator the size of a meat locker.

It's not that my brothers eat a lot (Mom says it's just a teenage phase), but once they've quit teenagerhood, I can guarantee you, world hunger will no longer be a problem. There'll be plenty of food for everyone.

Meanwhile, Dad wandered out to the garage to drool over Uncle Max's antique car collection.

And little Carrie was in the backyard, pointing at a tree, trying not to have a major stroke. "Look!" she cried. "There are oranges on this tree! There are oranges on this tree!"

"Well of course, Sweetheart, where did you think oranges came from?" Mom asked.

Carrie scrunched her face up into a puzzled frown. It was quite the brain sprain for her little seven-year-old mind to realize that oranges don't grow on grocery-store shelves.

I went up to one of the supercool guest bedrooms. Its balcony was bigger than my whole room back home. All of this excitement had really stirred up my creativity. Since we had a couple of hours to kill before going to watch Uncle Max, I pulled out ol' Betsy, my laptop computer, and started one of my superhero stories.

"Open a little farther, Mr. President."

"Ahhhh..."

"A little farther."

"Ahhhhhhhhh..."

"Perfect."

With the poise and grace of a true professional, the fabulously flexible and hygienically heroic Floss Man leaps into the president's mouth. Expertly he begins flossing between the great leader's teeth.

"Just a few more seconds, Mr. President."

"Uh-huh."

"Don't want unhealthy gums now, do we?"

"Uh-uh."

"Because as we all know, healthy gums are happy gu—"

RING, RING.
RING, RING.

Before our hero can rattle off that famous slogan found in every dentist office, the president turns to his desk and answers his phone.

"Hello?"

He tries to listen, but he can barely hear over the shouting inside his mouth.

"Miffer Preffibent! Oh, Miffer Preffibent!"

"I'm sorry," the president says into the phone, "you'll have to repeat that."

"Miffer Preffibent! Oh, Miffer Preffibent!"

"I'm sorry, can you wait just a minute?"

Then, with the genius only an elected official can have, the beloved leader opens his mouth and lets Floss Man leap out.

"Whew," our hero coughs and gasps. "Were those onions you had for lunch, sir?"

But the president is too busy to listen to bad breath jokes, especially from a piece of string—even if it is both mint flavored and waxed. He resumes his important phone conversation.

"You don't say," he says. "You don't say....You don't say."

Finally he hangs up and Floss Man asks, "What did he say?"

"He didn't say."

Before our hero can groan over that tired, old joke, the president suddenly puts his hands up to his eyes. "OWWW!"

"Mr. President, what's wrong? What's wrong?!"

"My eyes!"

"What about them? Let me see!"

But the president will not remove his hands. He continues to rub his eyes. Then Floss Man notices that the man's chubby round face is turning into a chubby square face. Not only that, but the rings on his chubby fingers are also turning into rectangles. And the round buttons on his jacket are becoming squares.

"Mr. President, what's going on?"

At last the president removes his hands, and our hero gasps a ghastly gasp.

"Mr. President, your eyeballs..."

"Yes..."

"They've become...(insert suspenseful music here)...eye*cubes!*"

"It's just as I feared!" the president cries. "Take a look!"

Quickly our hero scans the room. Everything round is growing corners. Three-ring notebooks are becoming three-hexagon notebooks. Doorknobs have become doorcubes. In fact, the entire Oval Office has now become, you guessed it...the Square Office.

"Great Scott, Mr. President! What's going on?"

"If our intelligence reports are accurate, it's the horrendous Harry the Hairball. Somehow he's giving corners to everything round."

"You're kidding!"

"Everything is turning square, Fl□ss Man. □h n□, l□□k at my w□rds. He's even changing the *□*s, I mean the *□*s. I mean—"

"I know, Mr. President, he's changing

your *o*s. But not mine. Look at my words. I can say all the *o*s I want. *O, o, o, o, o*—"

"That's because y□u're a string, Fl□ss Man, y□u're a straight line. Hairball can't t□uch y□u because there's n□thing r□und ab□ut y□u t□ t□uch!"

Then, just when this story couldn't get any weirder, or the print any stranger, a picture flickers up on the TV screen.

"Greetings bl□ckheads."

They spin around (make that spin a*square*) and see Harry the Hairball speaking. But instead of being round like any sensible hairball, he has more corners on him than a Rubik's Cube.

"In case y□u're w□ndering," he says, "I've released a t□xic gas int□ the atm□sphere. It is circling the gl□be, er, make that the cube—har, har, a little supervillain c□medy there. Even as we speak, it is attacking every r□und □bject. S□□n everything r□und will have c□rners. S□□n there will n□ l□nger be anything r□und!"

Once again he laughs a sinister laugh, which ends in a fit of coughing and hacking. (What did you expect from a Hairball, er Haircube?)

"Mr. President," our hero shouts, "what are you going to do?"

"There's n□thing I can d□. I can't m□ve."

"What?"

"It's n□t just my eyes, Fl□ss Man. It's everything ab□ut me. The balls □f my feet are n□w squares. The ball j□ints in my hips are cubes."

"But you can call your armies, launch your missiles!"

"Guns can't sh□□t square bullets. Missiles with c□rners can't fly. We're t□tally helpless, Fl□ss Man. There's □nly □ne pers□n wh□ can save us."

"You don't mean..." Suddenly there's a blast of superhero music (not to be confused with that earlier suspenseful music, though they're probably written by the same guy).

"That's right, Fl□ss Man, it's all up t□ y□u. Y□u're □ur □nly h□pe."

Before you have time to wonder how a piece of floss can move about (hey, this is a fantasy, remember?), our hero hops over to the nearest medicine cabinet. He

throws it open, jumps inside, and slips on his $19.95 cape and color-coordinated goggles. Then, after asking the mouthwash to swing by and give the president a little rinse (those onions are still working overtime), our hero emerges. He hops up to the windowsill, then leaps into the wind, only to discover—

"Hey, Wally!" It's Brock, shouting from downstairs. "Everybody's ready to go. Are you coming or what?"

I looked up from ol' Betsy and reached over to shut her down. I wasn't sure how Floss Man was going to save the day, but I wasn't about to miss how Uncle Max was.

* * * * *

"All right," the assistant director shouted through his megaphone. "Stand by please."

On the pier, we held our breath and leaned over the rail to get a better look at the water. Well, everyone but Dad. Water makes Dad nervous—real nervous. I don't want to say he's afraid of drowning, but he's the only person I know who takes a bath with a life preserver.

As you may remember from *My Life As Alien Monster Bait*, I'm an old pro at making movies (or at least destroying them). But this one was different. Way different.

First of all, I wasn't involved. This greatly increased its chances for success.

Second of all, that was my uncle in the water behind the ski boat.

And third, the world famous Arnold Swizzlenoggin was standing right beside me! Well, he *had* been standing beside me . . . until Uncle Max introduced us. I got so excited I spilled hot chocolate all over his pants. Then I tried to mop it up with my mustard-covered napkin, which was kind of useless. Then I bumped into Dad's arm and caused him to spill hot coffee all over Mr. Swizzlenoggin.

Nothing unusual for me. But for the rest of the evening, Mr. Swizzlenoggin kept my brothers, sister, and both of my parents between us.

Who could blame him? Even superheroes try not to risk their lives too many times a day.

But now the guy was shouting down to my Uncle Max. "Let's go, Max. . . . Make me look good, Max. Make me look good!"

Uncle Max grinned and gave him the thumbs up. We all waved back.

Dad shifted uneasily. I wondered if he was a

little jealous about his brother getting all of the attention.

"Quiet please," the director shouted.

We all settled down.

"And action, Max!"

The ski boat roared forward, pulling Uncle Max behind. In a second he was up on the water, skiing barefoot.

Meanwhile the pyrotechnic guys on the pier lit a fake tackle shop on fire.

WHOOSHHH . . .

A stunt woman, dressed like the leading lady, stood on top of the burning roof shouting, "Help me, Lance! Help me!"

I looked back to the boat. It was going full throttle and heading directly toward the pier.

"Help me, Lance! Help me!"

"Come on, Max," Swizzlenoggin shouted, "make me look good."

There was a miniature jump hidden behind a fake houseboat. Uncle Max swung wide and aimed for it.

"Help me, Lance! Oh, help me!"

"Make me look good, Max."

Uncle Max hit the ramp.

The crowd *oooed* as he shot up, sailing high into the air.

They *aahhed* as he let go of the towline and flew high over the pier toward the burning building.

And they *gaaasped* as he reached out, grabbed the stunt woman off the flaming roof, and continued over the pier, crashing into the water on the other side.

But the two of them barely hit the water before the burning tackle shack toppled over. It fell directly on them . . . along with a few hundred gallons of burning gasoline whose flames quickly spread out over the water.

Everyone waited breathlessly for Uncle Max and the woman to surface through the burning pieces of building and the flaming water. But they didn't show.

Five seconds passed.

Then ten.

People started to get nervous. Some began to mumble.

But not Dad. Unable to contain himself, good ol' Dad raced past the camera and right to the edge of the pier. "Somebody help him!"

"We're still rolling," the director screamed, "Get out of my picture! Get out of my picture!"

But Dad was doing his own brand of yelling. "That's my brother!" he cried. "Somebody's got to save him!"

Poor Dad. He just kept dancing along the edge of the pier, scared to death of the water and scared to death that his brother was dying. I knew he wanted to jump in. But I also knew he understood that his drowning wouldn't be a whole lot of help.

"Get out of my picture!" the director yelled. "Get out of my picture!"

"But that's my—"

Suddenly someone shouted. "There he is!"

We all turned to look.

Fifteen yards behind us, completely away from the flames, Uncle Max and the stunt woman had surfaced.

Everyone clapped and cheered.

Well, everyone but Dad.

. . . and the director.

"All right, folks," the director sighed. "I'm afraid we're going to have to do that again. This time *without* any help from the family."

A few people groaned. Some chuckled.

I threw a look at Dad. His face burned redder than the flames on the water below. What an embarrassment.

For him . . .

And for me.

Chapter 3

Fantasmo World

The next morning was full of cool. A cool view of the ocean, a cool breakfast, and of course, my incredibly cool Uncle Max.

But first I had to get past my uncool dad. As usual, he was up at the crack of dawn working. This time he was in his room going over all my great aunt's papers and stuff.

"Hey, Wally," he said as he saw me trying to sneak past.

"Hey, Dad," I said, trying not to look caught. It wasn't that I didn't want to be around him. I was just afraid he might bring up last night's disaster. When something that embarrassing happens, I've learned that it's better just to forget it and move on. And I should know. As the king of mishaps, I'm speaking from personal experience.

But Dad had something else on his mind. "When I'm done here," he said, "I was thinking maybe I could take everyone to where your Uncle Max and I grew up."

"Sure," I said, trying to sound excited (though I rated the adventure right up there with emptying the cat box). Fortunately a perfect excuse came to mind. "But weren't we going to watch Uncle Max's show at Fantasmo World and go on some of the rides and stuff?"

"Oh, that's right," Dad said. "Well, then maybe we could do it tomorrow."

"Sounds great," I lied as I turned and headed down the hall as fast as I could. If I'd hung around, he'd probably have come up with an even niftier idea, like going to the dentist to have our teeth drilled.

I found Uncle Max and my brothers down in the weight room. It figured. Dad was in his room pushing a pencil, and Uncle Max was in the weight room with Burt and Brock pumping iron. How could Max and Dad be so different? One lived a life of nonstop excitement; the other a life that would cure insomnia.

"Want to join us?" Uncle Max asked.

"You bet," I exclaimed.

I'll tell you, it was quite a workout. First I had to get my shirt over my head. Then I had to struggle getting my arms out of the sleeves. Then finally

I was able to pull off the ol' shirt. Whew, talk about working up a sweat.

But Uncle Max thought I should "push the envelope" and actually work out with weights, too.

"How 'bout some bench presses?" he asked.

"Bench presses?"

"Sure, it'll help build up that chest and those upper arms."

I nodded and eagerly sat down on the bench. I couldn't wait to get back home and show off my brand-new muscles . . . well, at least one or two . . . well, all right, maybe a tiny fraction of a very small one.

"Do you do this a lot?" I asked.

"Couple of hours a day," he said. "Then of course there's the running, swimming, and the time in the tanning booth."

"Every day?"

"Oh yeah. Hey, check these out."

He gave a flex and about a hundred muscles popped out on his arm.

"Wow," I said.

"Now, slide under the barbell and get ready to lift it off the stand."

I lay down on my back and scooted under the barbell.

"I'm surprised your dad doesn't do this type of

stuff," Uncle Max said. He pulled some weights off the barbell to make it lighter for me. "No offense, but he's beginning to get a bit of a gut on him."

"Yeah," I said, reaching up to the bar. "Of course he's way too busy going to work, helping at church, and running us wherever we have to go."

Uncle Max shook his head. "Doesn't sound like much of a life."

"You got that right," I said, feeling just a little bit like a traitor. After all, we were talking about my dad.

"I mean what does the guy do for fun?"

"Fun," I said as I tried push the barbell off the stand. "Dad doesn't have fun. Dad's a . . . well, he's a dad. The high point of his week is a snooze on the couch."

Uncle Max shook his head again. "Sure isn't my idea of a life."

"Yeah," I agreed. I pushed even harder. "You're sure not going to catch me living like that when I grow up and—"

But before I could finish my Benedict Arnold imitation, the barbell fell off the stand and

"AUGHHH!!!"
CLUNK!

The "*AUGHHH!!!*" was me screaming.

The *CLUNK* was the barbell smashing down on my chest.

"Get it off!" I cried. "It's crushing me!"

"Push it up, Wally. Push."

"It's too heavy!"

"Push!"

"Take off more weight. You've got too much—"

"Wally."

"You've got too much weight—"

"WALLACE!"

His tone brought me to a stop. I looked up and saw that he was pointing to the ends of the barbell. There wasn't a single weight on either end. The bar was completely empty.

"Maybe we better start off with something a little less challenging," he suggested.

"Yeah," I croaked, "that might be better." I wasn't sure if I was feeling like an idiot because of my outstanding display of dork-oidness . . . or because I was putting down my dad.

Maybe it was a little of both.

Unfortunately, a little would soon turn into a lot. . . .

* * * * *

Fantasmo World was incredible. It had all sorts of rides and shows and stuff. And plenty of cartoon types wandered around, like Crystal Bright and the Seven Dweebs—Stinky, Cranky, Dorky, Dippy, Jerko, Drooly, and Nerdly. Then, of course, there were Rabid Rabbit, Maniac Mouse, Slobester and Twit Bird, and all the rest of the Saturday morning TV gang.

And the employees—everywhere you looked there was some employee smiling at you.

"What's wrong with them?" Burt asked.

"Got me," Brock answered.

"It's like their faces are permanently frozen," Burt said.

"If you ask me, they're all a few fries short of a Happy Meal," Brock chuckled.

"Hee, hee, hee, that's a good one, Brock."

"Check this out," Brock said as he approached an overhappy employee. "Excuse me? Miss?"

She turned to him, all grins.

"I'm sorry to break the news to you," Brock said, "but your grandmother just got run over by a Mac truck."

"Well, thank you for sharing," the employee said, grinning so big I thought she'd sprain her lips. "And be sure to have a fan-fan-fantastic day here at Fantasmo World, allrighteee?"

We all looked at each other then broke out laughing.

Of course, all the bigwigs at the park knew Uncle Max, which meant free rides, free shows, even free food . . . which managed to perk up Dad's smiler a bit.

Unfortunately he wasn't smiling at the Schmuzo Killer Whale show. That's when the host (another good friend of Uncle Max's) just happened to select Dad from the audience to stand beside the tank.

Everyone, including Dad, gasped as Schmuzo leaped high into the air.

Everyone *but* Dad laughed when Schmuzo belly flopped into the tank and splashed about a billion gallons of water on him.

It's not that Dad can't take a joke, it's just hard to laugh when you're busy coughing, choking, and drowning. He did manage to throw a look at Uncle Max. It really wasn't much of a smile. More like one of those pathetic you-know-I'm-afraid-of-water-so-why-are-you-trying-to-kill-me kind of looks.

Of course, Uncle Max was having too good a time to notice. But I did. And, though I pretended to laugh with the other 1,200 audience members, I was growing more and more embarrassed about having Dad as . . . well, about having him as my dad.

Later, when the show was over, Uncle Max wanted to take us underground.

"Underground?" Mom asked.

"That's right," he said. "Not many people know it, but there's an entire network of tunnels running beneath the park. It's like a complete city under there."

"Won't we miss your show?" Dad asked.

"Nah, it's not until this afternoon. We have plenty of time to grab something to eat and check out the tunnels. Then, when I'm suiting up for the show, you guys can take in a few rides."

We all agreed. I put down a lunch of two chocolate-covered bananas, a family-sized box of caramel corn, and a I-think-I'm-going-to-hurl-if-I-have-to-eat-this-fifth-corn-dog corn dog (hey, the eats were free, remember?). Then I grabbed a giant econo-sized cherry/orange/root beer Slusho-Ice, and we followed Uncle Max across the park.

There were all sorts of cool rides from different movies: *Riders of the Last Bark* (where archaeologists discover a giant dog and ride on it), *Star Wreck*, *Honey I Shrunk Your Underwear*, *Beauty and the Fleas*, and of course, *The Examinator* (where a school teacher goes crazy during test week).

"Wow," I said, looking all around and still slurping my Slusho-Ice. "You get to work here every day?"

"That's right." Uncle Max beamed.

"I bet you wish you could work in a place like this, huh Daddy," little Carrie said.

Dad kind of squirmed and shrugged. "Oh I don't know, my office isn't so bad."

"Yeah, right," Burt smirked. "Your office is a great place for nonstop, action-packed boredom."

Immediately Carrie came to Dad's defense. "Well, I think it's a pretty building," she said, taking his hand.

"Thank you, Sweetheart."

"Even if you don't ever do anything cool and neat like Uncle Max."

We hardly noticed Dad wince as Uncle Max led us to a giant tree. "This will only take a few minutes," he said as he twisted a branch. Suddenly a door popped open, right out of the back of the trunk.

"Cool," we all said.

"Come on, follow me."

We were pretty impressed as we followed him into the tree and walked down a steep spiral staircase. Well, everyone else walked. I was busy doing my best falling routine.

BANG-BOUNCE-TUMBLE . . . SPLAT

The *banging, bouncing*, and *tumbling* were, of course, my soft little body on the not-so-soft stairs.

But I couldn't place the *SPLAT* . . . until I looked up from the floor and saw Uncle Max's face.

I gasped.

"Nice job," Uncle Max said, carefully wiping off my Slusho-Ice.

"I'm sorry," I cried, expecting him to blow up.

"Don't worry about it." He grinned as he grabbed the paper cone from my hand and dumped the Slusho-Ice back into it. "It can get pretty warm down here. Thanks for helping to keep me cool."

It was just a little thing, but it proved how incredible this guy was. Not only was he super-rich and superfamous, but he also knew how to have a super good time and stay supercool (in more ways than one).

I couldn't help glancing at Dad. The difference was so obvious, it was painful. I mean, if the Slusho-Ice had hit Dad, he would have given me a week-long lecture about being more careful. I know this sounds lousy and everything, but a part of me actually wished that Uncle Max could have been my dad.

Of course, I felt pretty guilty and tried to shrug it off. But the thought just kept coming back.

We headed down the tunnel and saw lots of other tunnels branching off in different directions. I guess they weren't really tunnels. They were more like hallways with rounded ceilings made out of smooth concrete. And they were lit as brightly as any office building.

We passed other employees. Of course, they all knew my uncle. "Hi, Max." "Good afternoon, Mr. McDoogle." "Have a great show, Max."

There were also plenty of folks dressed up like cartoon characters. Most of them carried their cartoon heads under their arms.

"Hey, Max."

We turned to see a giant Sasquatch approach. He was about seven feet tall. He had long apelike arms and stringy brown fur. Except for his human head, he could have easily passed for a real Bigfoot monster.

"Oh, hi, Sid," Uncle Max said. Then after introducing us, he explained that Sid was the main bad guy in his stunt show.

"That's what I gots to talk to ya about," Sid said. "I think Julie's comin' down with the flu."

"She'll still be able to do the show, won't she?" Uncle Max asked.

"Maybe today's show, but we'll need a replacement for tomorrow."

"What about her understudy?" Uncle Max asked.

"Gots an out of town job this week."

"Great," Uncle Max sighed. "Well, we need somebody."

Sid the Sasquatch glanced down at me, then grinned. "Your nephew here's about the right size." Max turned and looked at me as Bigfoot asked, "What say, son? Feel like being my helpless victim for tomorrow's show?"

My eyes shot up to Uncle Max. "Can I?! I mean is that possible?"

Uncle Max broke into a smile. "I don't know why not. I've noticed that you're pretty good at screaming and falling down."

"I practice all the time."

Dad cleared his throat. "I'm not so sure, Max. I mean is that sort of thing safe?"

I rolled my eyes. There was Dad again, busy being a dad.

"Of course it's safe," Max said.

Dad scowled.

"Don't be such a worrywart, Herbie. He'll be in less danger doing the show than riding home on the freeway."

"Particularly if he's riding with Max," Sid teased.

"Can I, Dad?" I asked. "Can I?"

"I don't know. . . . Your mother and I need to talk about it."

I had two choices. I could stomp my foot and

sulk—which stopped working about the time I turned four. Or I could pretend to be an adult and wait.

I voted for the latter. The rest of the underground tour went by in a blur. All I could think about was starring in a real live stunt show with Uncle Max. And if all I had to do was fall down a lot, I mean, let's face it, I'd been preparing to play that part all my life.

I don't remember a lot of the tour. But I do remember going into a giant computer room that controlled all the rides. It had tons of monitors and more flashing lights than the latest *Star Trek* movie. I also remembered that I no longer had the rest of my melting Slusho-Ice.

I must have set it down on one of the computer consoles when I tied my shoe. I just don't remember if I picked it up and threw it away. Maybe I forgot and left it there to melt on top of the computer. . . .

I didn't know then, but unfortunately, I'd know soon.

Chapter 4

The Ride of a Lifetime

We still had a couple of hours to kill before Uncle Max's stunt show, so we hit the rides. Of course Burt and Brock wanted to go on all of the stand-in-line-for-three-days-and-then-have-to-leave-just-when-you-get-to-the-front-'cause-you-have-to-go-to-the-restroom rides.

But since I've got a touchy stomach (I break out in a bad case of puke-itis just watching the ceiling fan in our living room go around), we decided to split up. The twins and Dad went one direction; Carrie, Mom, and I headed another.

I knew it was risky business hanging out with a seven-year-old. If I wasn't careful, I'd wind up on one of those lame flying animal rides or on some enchanted boat voyage. (The scariest part is wondering if you'll die from boredom.)

So, before she had a chance to think, I quickly pointed out some cool gas-powered cars. The miniature highway wound all over the place. "Let's check those out," I said.

She wrinkled her nose. "They're just stupid cars."

"I know, but I'll be getting my license in a few years and—"

"If you live through the seventh grade," she reminded me.

I nodded. "Exactly, and if I don't, this will be the closest I ever get to driving before I die. You wouldn't want to deprive me of that, would you?"

It was a long shot, so I had to put a little catch in my voice and a tear in my eye.

Luckily, she fell for it. (Seven-year-olds can be so gullible.) Ten minutes later, an attendant buckled Carrie and me into a gas-powered, two-seater mini sports car.

Unfortunately Mom stood off to the side, wringing her hands and doing her mom thing.

"Are you sure those are safe?" she called out to the attendant.

I glanced around in embarrassment. "Mom . . ."

"Absolutely," the attendant called back. "There's a bar running down the center of the road, so the car can't go off."

"What about speed?" she shouted.

"Mom . . ."

"They have their own gas pedal. But if the cars

get going too fast, a remote radio signal kicks in and takes over."

"What if they have to stop for a potty brea—"

"MOM, PLEASE . . ."

She gave me a weak smile. "You're right. Sorry."

"Don't worry, ma'am," the attendant called back. "Kids have been riding these for years without a single accident."

That did little to ease Mom's fears. After all, he'd never seen the World President of Dork-oids Anonymous behind the wheel.

The attendant gave us a running push and said, "Have a fan-fan-fantastic ride at Fantasmo World."

And we were off.

What an experience! That powerful 3/4 horse engine throbbed under the hood. The wind flew through my hair. The trees blurred as we raced—

"C'mon Wally," Carrie complained, "I can walk faster than this."

"All right, all right." I tromped on the accelerator. Raw power surged through the vehicle. The acceleration pushed us deep into our seats. Before I knew it, we were up to 3 1/2, maybe even 4 miles an hour.

And then it happened. Little did I know it then, but my melting Slusho-Ice down in the master control room had been working overtime. Carefully it had melted its way deep into the inner workings of the computer system, until finally . . .

"Wally, what's wrong with that music?"

I gave a listen. It was the same silly theme song that had played ever since we arrived:

It's Fantasmo after all,
It's Fantasmo after all,
It's Fantasmo after all,
It's a Fan-fan-tasmo World.

But now it was going so fast it sounded like the singing Chipmunks breathing helium. Faster and faster it played. Higher and higher the voices rose.

But it wasn't only the music that was going faster . . .

"Look at that!" I pointed.

Overhead, the sky ride had also picked up speed. Some of the people on board had started to panic. Others began to scream.

"And over there!" Carrie pointed to the nearby merry-go-round. It had started to spin so fast that people had to fight to hang on.

Thanks to my time-released Slusho-Ice, melting goo had shorted out the computer, making everything go faster.

Everything including us.

"Slow down, Wally! Slow down!"

"I'm trying," I shouted as I hit the brakes for the hundredth time. But nothing happened.

Cars raced by. Some of the kids in them were screaming. Others were crying.

"Slow down, Wally! You're scaring me!"

"I'm scaring *you*? What about *me*?"

The faster we went, the harder it was to steer. Now it's true, my eye-hand coordination isn't the best. (I hold the world's record for the greatest number of quarters lost per video game. Translation: I usually crash those jet fighter planes before they even get off the ground.) But this was ridiculous. If it wasn't for that bar running down the middle of the road, there was no way we could have stayed on the track.

And still we picked up speed.

Carrie began screaming nonstop. As far as I could tell, she didn't even take time out to breathe.

Faster and faster the road raced by.

Faster and faster my life flashed before my eyes.

And then I saw it. Actually, we both saw it.

"It's a hairpin curve!" Carrie screamed. "Turn, Wally, turn!"

"I'm turning. I'm turning."

I cranked that wheel as far to the left as possible. Unfortunately, the roadway turned to the right.

SCRAAAAAPE . . .
SCREEEEECH . . .
K-BAM!

I'm not sure how it happened. But we were going fast—so fast that our car jumped the metal bar down the center of the road, and we flew off the track.

The good news was we were no longer on the ride that had gone berserk. The bad news was we were still in a car going berserk.

Going berserk and picking up speed . . .

First there were the bushes and shrubs.

K-THWACK, K-THWACK . . .
SCRRREEEEEEEAAMMMMM!

(Thank you Carrie, I didn't need to use that ear again, anyway.)

Then we raced down the main street of Fantasmo World. "Get out of the way!" I yelled. "Get out of the way! Get out of the—"

K-SMACK, K-SMACK, K-SMACK.

Those of course were the slow pedestrians and

"AUGGHHHH!"
RRRRIIIIIIP . . .

the Galactic Space Queen, strolling down the street in her long flowing robes. Well, she *had* been in long flowing robes. Now they were trailing off our front bumper, and she was running for the nearest bushes.

But, the fun and games had barely begun.

"There's Daddy!" Carrie pointed. "And Burt and Brock!"

I turned my head just in time to see them standing in the long line we were zooming past.

And our brothers, being so kind and extremely intelligent, immediately began to scream, "Hey, no cuts! No cuts!"

I faced forward again and saw why they were concerned. We were heading directly into the most popular ride in the park—the Castle of Horrors.

"I'm not old enough to go on this ride!" Carrie screamed.

"I wish I wasn't," I shouted. "Look out!" I waved at the ticket takers. "Look out!"

They leaped off the drawbridge and into the moat. I would have offered them a towel (or at least a nice Galactic Space Queen robe), but we were too busy crashing through the castle's gate to be polite.

First up was the cobwebbed entrance hall, complete with all sorts of goblins and ghosts reflected in a giant mirror.

CRASH! TINKLE-TINKLE-TINKLE . . .

Well, they had been in the mirror. Now I hoped they could find some good low-rent housing to relocate to.

Next came the suits of armor. I don't want to say we destroyed all of them. But if you ever need spare parts for a pot-bellied stove or armored tank, or just want to re-side your house in sheet metal, feel free to give me a call.

Next came the banquet hall, music room, and library. I'll save you the gory details. But if you call that same number, we'll throw in legs of lamb, piano keys (your choice of white or black), and more books than a bookstore.

Of course I was still trying to steer, but that was pretty pointless. After destroying most of the castle, we headed up a giant circular staircase, wh-wh-wh-ich wa-wa-was pr-pr-pre-ty-ty-ty bum-bum-bum-py-py-py. Then I turned left instead of right (so what else is new?), and

K-RASH!

We smashed through a giant stained-glass window.

The good news was we were finally out of that creepy haunted castle. The bad news was we were sailing fifty feet above the ground. But as luck would have it, we didn't fall all the way back down. Oh no, that would have been too easy (except for the doctor bills). Instead,

CA-LANG!

We landed directly on the rails to the world's biggest roller coaster.

Now, I don't want to say it's a scary ride. But I've heard that as you wait in line, the overhead monitors give a crash course in CPR, just in case your neighbor's heart decides to stop.

"Do something!" my sister screamed. "Do something!"

"I have been!" I shouted.

"Then stop doing something!"

The car stayed glued to the tracks as we went down and up and down and up and down and up. The only trouble was, when I was going down, my stomach was going up . . .

And up . . .

And up . . .

And . . .

Then, just when my lunch was about to make a return appearance (and believe me, those corn dogs weren't so great the first time around), we finally leveled off.

But not for long.

We began to head back up. Higher and higher and higher we rose. I'm not going to complain and say we were too high. But I do remember having to duck when we passed under the moon. Finally, mercifully, the tracks stopped sloping up.

That was the good news.

The bad news was they started sloping down.

I opened my mouth to scream. Unfortunately, the only thing that came out was . . .

I tried again. I opened my mouth and . . .

Still nothing.

I guess the sound of a scream doesn't catch up if you're falling faster than the speed of sound. (See how educational these disasters can be?)

Figuring I'd be meeting God in the next couple of seconds, I closed my eyes and asked Him to forgive me for everything I'd ever done wrong. I'd just gotten to smoking those crayons behind the garage at age six when I felt Carrie's elbow dig into my ribs.

"Not now Carrie."

She dug harder.

"Carrie, I said not—"

But I could tell she was pretty serious (either that or she was practicing to be an open-heart surgeon). So I opened my eyes.

I wished I hadn't.

There, coming up the same tracks we were going down was a roller coaster full of people.

They screamed.

We screamed.

We were thirty feet away and closing in rapidly.

They screamed some more.

We screamed some more.

Twenty feet.

I was getting a little bored with all the screaming, so I dreamed up something new.

Fifteen feet.

Something exciting and original.

Ten.

Like trying to save our lives.

Five.

I cranked the wheel hard to the right.

The wheels screeched, scraped, and scranked (don't ask), and we sailed off the tracks just as the roller coaster roared by.

Once again we were flying through the air.

I looked down. Below and to the right was the three-story Flaming Inferno attraction.

"Lean to the right," I shouted.

"What?" Carrie cried.

"Lean to the right. If we hit that building down there, it will break our fall."

Carrie nodded. We leaned for all we were worth.

"Harder," I shouted. "Harder!"

It was close, but somehow we caught the edge of the roof. We hit it hard, bounced a bunch of times, and finally slid to a stop.

We were safe. It had taken some doing, but I had saved our lives. Imagine that. Me, Wally the hero. Me, Wally the super driver. Me, Wally the—

"Moron!" cried Carrie.

"What?"

"Look what you've done."

"I know what I've done. I've just saved your life by landing on this building. The least you could do is show your thanks."

"For what? Turning us into a human barbecue?"

"What are you talking about?"

"Look, Wally. This whole building. It's on fire!"

Chapter 5

Dad to the Rescue . . . Almost

Of course I knew the building wasn't really burning. It was just a movie set, an attraction people paid money to see. Oh, sure the flames were real, but they were fed by little gas nozzles. The building wasn't really—

"Wally, our car's burning!"

I spun around to look. One of those little gas nozzles must have ignited our little back end. No problem, except that little back end was connected to a little gas engine that was connected to a little gas tank that could easily—

"Run!" I cried, "it's going to blow!"

Carrie didn't have to be told twice. Neither did I. We leaped out of the car and headed for cover. We'd barely scampered behind some giant vents near the edge of the roof when suddenly

K-WHOOOOOSH!

Our little car made a not-so-little explosion.

We ducked as bits and pieces of burning car rained down around us. And then, to our amazement we heard . . . applause.

Carrie and I glanced at each other then looked over the edge of our burning building. There, three stories below us, an audience stood applauding and nodding in approval.

"What are they doing?" Carrie shouted.

"They think we're part of the show!" I yelled.

I couldn't believe it. Here we were, barely escaping an exploding car, surrounded by flames, about to become crispy critters, and everybody thought we were part of the show.

Well, not quite everybody . . .

Having seen everything from the Castle of Horrors line, Dad had raced toward the Flaming Inferno. He leaped over the handrail and started climbing the charred and smoldering building.

"Hang on, kids, I'm coming."

"Oh no," I groaned, "what's he going to mess up now?"

Of course the crowd only *ooed* and *aahed.* They thought the show was getting more suspenseful.

"Be careful, Daddy!" Carrie screamed.

Dad nodded and continued working his way up through the building. His face and clothes blackened, he ignored the flames flickering on all sides and just kept climbing. I was pretty impressed. For an old man, he was making good progress. So far he'd gotten about six and a half feet off the ground.

"Any time Dad," I muttered as the flames licked all around us. "Any time."

Suddenly there was a loud

CREAK . . . CRASH!

Part of the roof near us caved in and fell away.

WHOOOOOOSHHHH . . .

Even more flames leaped up and surrounded us.

"Hurry, Daddy, hurry!"

I watched in stunned amazement. The pain on Dad's face made it pretty clear that his back had given out again. But he wouldn't stop. The guy just kept on coming. Unfortunately, it didn't matter a whole lot. He'd only climbed about fifteen feet when he made a major mistake.

"No, not that one!" I shouted as he jumped toward a beam. "The top is burnt, it can't hold your—"

Suddenly it gave way. It slipped and tipped violently, throwing Dad to his knees. He slid all the way to its edge.

"DADDY!" Carrie screamed.

How embarrassing, I thought.

Still, he managed to cling to the end.

More applause.

Now, all three of us were in danger. Dad about to plunge to the hard pavement below. Carrie and I about to become charcoal briquettes.

And then, suddenly: "Hang on, you two!"

We looked up. "Uncle Max!"

With mountain gear, he had dropped down from the roller coaster supports to join us.

"Here," he shouted, "take these straps. Wrap them around your waists and buckle onto me."

We followed his instructions. After a few fumblings (what else is new?), I finally managed to buckle us in.

"Okay," he ordered, "hang on."

We nodded and clung to him as he pushed off. He effortlessly took us down the front of the burning building. In a matter of seconds all three of us had landed safely on the ground.

There was plenty of clapping and cheering. And already we could hear little voices begging, "Let's see this ride again, Mommy, let's see it again!"

Of course Uncle Max paid no attention. He had other things on his mind. He quickly spun around and started to climb back up to rescue Dad. I'm sure Max thought he was doing Dad a favor. But from the look of humiliation on Dad's face, I figured he might have been happier to have just been left there to die.

* * * * *

An hour later, we headed back to Uncle Max's place. The park officials had decided to shut Fantasmo World down for the rest of the day.

"So what exactly went wrong?" Burt asked.

"Dunno," Uncle Max said. "But somebody found a Slusho-Ice on top of the master computer."

The words *Slusho-Ice* and *computer* brought back some vivid memories. Hadn't I had a Slusho-Ice? Hadn't I been in the computer room? It was an absurd thought, so I pushed it from my mind. Besides, what could a little Slusho-Ice do?

"Looks like it melted right into the computer," Max continued. "It shorted out the whole system."

My stomach started doing little flip-flops.

"Now, who would be stupid enough to leave something like that on a computer?" Brock asked.

"Got me. But whoever it was has strange taste buds. The giant Slusho-Ice was part cherry, orange, and root beer."

My stomach had gone from flip-flops into major

somersaults and tumbling. I was even thinking about entering it in the Olympics when I noticed that Dad hadn't said a single word. He just sat silently beside me, staring out the car window.

"You all right?" I asked.

No answer.

"Dad?"

"Huh?" He coughed and pretended to clear his throat. "Yeah, uh," he gave a sniff, "it's just my stupid allergies acting up again."

But by the way he kept staring out the window, I knew it was more than allergies. He had major hurt feelings. And I knew why. The last little event at the Flaming Inferno had been pretty humiliating for him. In fact, the whole trip had been. Seems like every time he turned around, Uncle Max was doing things a thousand times better than he was.

But it wasn't Uncle Max's fault. You couldn't blame him for staying in California and making something out of himself. It wasn't Uncle Max's fault that he was everybody's hero. And it definitely wasn't Uncle Max's fault that Dad was so . . . you, know . . . uncool.

I hated thinking it, but it was the truth. Like it or not, Uncle Max was right. Dad was a loser.

Once we got home, we put down another incredible dinner, courtesy of Uncle Max's cook. Then, to help forget the day I scrambled up to my room, snapped on ol' Betsy, and got back to my superhero story.

When we last left Floss Man, he was about to leap out of the president's window. He had to stop Harry the Haircube from releasing the toxic gas that's adding corners to everything round.

No one's sure what made Harry such a corner freak. Some say it's because his mother made him eat three *square* meals a day. Others say it's because he was nearly run over by a bowling ball as a baby.

Then there's the theory that his school teacher made him drink *OVAL*tine and eat little round crackers for every snack, every week, for a whole year. Whatever the reason, Harry hated curves in every shape and form.

Anyway, Floss Man stands at the windowsill and takes a deep breath. With a harrowing heroic lunge, our heroic hero heroically leaps. (Translation: The guy jumps.)

Faster and faster he falls, fluttering through the air. All the while he's hoping against hope that through some very clever writing, the wind will pick up his little thread body and carry him to Haircube's headquarters.

Unfortunately, our writer is not that clever.

Unfortunatelier, the little thread body is suddenly caught in the beak of a not-so-little robin.

Unfortunateliest, Ms. Red Breast thinks she's going to use him as part of her nest.

"Put me down," our hero shouts. "Put me down!"

"Cheep, cheep," Bird Brain chirps.

"I said put me down!"

"Cheep, cheep," she repeats.

Well, that about wraps up any chance for intelligent conversation. This poor feathered creature couldn't pour water out of a pitcher with the instructions on the bottom.

Desperately Floss Man looks for a way out. He glances to the ground below and sees that things are worse than he thought. *Everything* is growing corners. Cars are skidding and sliding on square wheels. Folks are choking on their breakfasts of Cheerios—make that Cheeri*squares*. And children are knocking themselves silly trying to twirl square hula hoops.

Once again Floss Man shouts to the bird. "You don't understand! Haircube is putting corners on everything."

"Cheep, cheep," Ms. Red Breast says.

"If you're thinking of using me to build your nest, you've got some major worries ahead."

"Cheep, cheep?" she asks.

"Why? I'll tell you why. If you're building a nest, you're going to be laying eggs."

"Cheep, cheep."

"Any idea how much fun laying square eggs will be?"

Immediately the robin changes her attitude, as well as her direction.

"All right!" Floss Man shouts. "Take me to Haircube's, on the double."

Faster than you can ask yourself how a bird can understand English, they are over Haircube's hideout. Once an M & M's factory, it is now reduced to making little candy cubes (those new blue ones are pretty tasty).

"Take me to that smokestack over there, the one belching out all that toxic gas. Drop me into—"

Before he can even finish his request, Bird Brain darts to the smokestack and drops Floss Man inside.

CRASH! RATTLE...
COUGH, COUGH, COUGH.

He flutters to the bottom. But when Floss Man throws open the smokestack door and steps into the factory, he is met by the hideous sight of—

"Hey, Wally!" Uncle Max shouted. "Shut that thing off. If you're doing the show with me tomorrow, you'll need your rest."

All right! The show. With all that had happened, I'd almost forgotten.

If I had known what was in store for me, I'd wished I had.

Chapter 6

Breakfast Acrobatics

Breakfast was interesting, to say the least.

Actually it was interesting, to say the most too.

First there were Burt and Brock, the human eating machines. Uncle Max hadn't come downstairs yet, but yesterday he'd said they could eat as much as they could hold. Right now it looked like they were going for some sort of world's record.

"Would you *BELCH* pass that fifth plate of *BURP* French toast *BELCH?"* Burt asked.

"If you'll *BURP* pass that sixth platter of *BELCH* eggs *BURP,"* Brock answered.

Then of course there was little Carrie, who went into fits every time a piece of food on her plate touched another piece.

"The syrup's touching my eggs! The syrup's touching my eggs!"

"I'm sorry, Sweetheart," Mom said, "but there's nothing I can do."

"Towel them off! Get the hair dryer!"

Then of course there was Dad, still reading and studying our great aunt's paperwork.

"Herb," Mom said while pouring him another cup of coffee. (Well, it was supposed to be coffee. But since it was the cook's day off and since Uncle Max's coffee maker was kind of new to Mom, it looked more like melted tar.) "You've been up all night working on that, why don't you give it a rest?"

He took off his glasses and rubbed his eyes. "I'd love to," he sighed, "but if I don't do this, who will?"

"She was Max's aunt too. Why won't he help?"

"Since when has Max helped with anything?" Dad asked.

"Uncle Max is busy," I said, coming to his defense. "He doesn't have time for little things like that."

"Of course he doesn't," Dad sighed as he returned to his paperwork. "Uncle Max doesn't have time for anybody but Uncle Max."

The comment bugged me. I mean it was obvious Dad was just jealous. But before I could say anything, the French doors in the dining room exploded into a zillion pieces.

Mom screamed.

Burt and Brock belched.

Carrie complained about the flying splinters of wood touching her bacon.

And two men of the thug variety burst in.

"Where is he?" Thug One shouted.

"Now see here," Dad said, rising to his feet. "What do you think you're doing? You can't come bursting in here and—"

That was as far as he got before Thug Two shoved a small revolver in his face. (It's hard to talk with your mouth wrapped around the barrel of a small revolver.)

"That ain't him," Thug One shouted. "Where is he? Where's Max McDoogle?"

But before any of us could turn informer, Uncle Max appeared in his robe on the balcony above us.

"What's all the noise down—uh, oh." Without another word, he spun around and sprinted back down the hall.

Now, the way I figured it, he was either going to jump into the shower to freshen up for our breakfast guests . . . or he was running for his life. And by the way the thugs started after him, I voted for the latter.

In a flash, they dashed up the stairs and disappeared after him. In another flash, Max suddenly dropped from a window onto the lawn in front of the dining room. He headed inside to join us while hopping up and down trying to get his legs into his pants.

"Who are those people?" Dad shouted.

"The guys trying to collect on my gambling debts," Uncle Max said as he continued to hop. "Say, are you going to eat this toast, Herb?"

Dad shook his head. Uncle Max grabbed it, crammed it into his mouth, and hopped for the door.

"Oh, Wally," he said spinning around. "Rehearsal at 10:00 this morning. Don't be late."

I nodded.

He wrinkled his nose and glanced at his toast. "Herbie, you've got to cut down on the butter. Not very good for your health."

Suddenly the thugs appeared on the balcony.

"After him!" they shouted as they started down the stairs.

Speaking of health, Uncle Max decided now would be a good time to dash out the front door. Not, of course, without being the polite host and encouraging us all to "have a nice day."

* * * * *

An hour later I was upstairs getting ready for my world debut as a stunt man at Fantasmo World. There wasn't much I could do except pack a hundred bandages (just in case my klutziness acted up) and throw in a pair of crutches. Then, of course, there was the call to 911 to put them on standby, and a message to the nearest funeral home, just in case. (I like to be prepared.)

I was putting the finishing touches on my last will and testament when there was a knock on the door.

"Come in."

It was Mom. "Hey, Wally."

"Hi."

Pause.

"So you're getting all ready to go to Fantasmo World and rehearse with Uncle Max."

"Yup."

Pause.

"Should be fun," she said.

"Yup."

Another pause.

Now you don't have to be a brain surgeon to know that when Mom lets all those pauses slip in, she's got something on her mind. You also don't have to be a genius to figure out that she expects you to ask what it is. So, being the nongenius that I am, I did.

"What's up, Mom?"

"Well . . . I know your father wouldn't come up here and say this. That's not his way, but . . ."

Pause.

I glanced at my watch. "Mom, it's getting kinda late. Can we skip the pauses?"

She nodded. "Do you remember when Dad said he wanted to show us where he grew up?"

I nodded.

"Well, since we're leaving tomorrow, this morning would be the last chance."

"But I've got rehearsal in half an hour, and then the show this afternoon."

"I know. And I'd hate for you to miss it. But—"

I could see where she was going and tried to cut her off at the pass. "Mom, this is a chance of a lifetime."

"I know . . . it's just . . . well, it would mean so much to your father. He'd love to show us around his old neighborhood and tell us stories of his childhood . . ."

She let another pause slip in just for good measure, but I wasn't falling for it. This time I let the silence hang.

She gave a long, quiet sigh.

Uh-oh, red alert, red alert. She's going for the guilt. She's going for the guilt.

It took every ounce of my strength, but I was able to hold my ground and not say a word.

Finally she rose from the bed. "I suppose you're right, Sweetheart. It would be selfish to ask you to miss out on that show . . . after all . . ." another sigh. *Uh-oh, here it comes . . .* "What's he ever done for you?"

"Oh, Mom . . ."

She flashed me a grin. "That was a little much, wasn't it?"

I grinned back. "I'll say. Especially after what he's put me through these last couple of days."

"What do you mean?"

"Let's face it. Dad's been nothing but an embarrassment this whole trip."

Mom hesitated, then crossed over and shut the door. She turned back to me. I could tell by the way her voice quivered that she was pretty upset. "Don't say that. Don't you ever say that."

Her tone surprised me, and I tried to explain. "Well, that's all he is. I mean why couldn't he be like Uncle Max—"

"Wally."

But I was on a roll and couldn't stop. "Why couldn't he be Mr. Cool, with all the cars, the money, the superstar friends. I mean Uncle Max is practically a hero, and Dad's just . . . well, he's just . . ."

"He's just what, Wally?"

"Well, you know." I shrugged. "He's kind of a loser."

Mom grabbed me by the arm and sat me down

on the bed . . . hard. "Don't you dare say that about your father!"

I looked at her and blinked.

"Your father's more of a hero than your Uncle Max will ever be."

I looked at her like she had a screw loose.

She continued. "Oh sure, he may not be in the limelight or have the fancy home and expensive things. But he's there for us day and night. Whenever we need him, your father is there for us."

"But Mom, he's just a—"

"Do you know how tough it is to raise a family these days? Do you? To work your fingers to the bone, to make sure your children have food to eat, clothes to wear, a roof over their heads? Do you have any idea what it's like to always put your wife and kids first and yourself last?"

I wanted to interrupt, but I could see Mom had a pretty good head of steam, so I held my tongue.

"Do you know why we came out here?"

"Because we finally begged him to death?" I offered.

She didn't even hear me. "We came out here because your Uncle Max wouldn't organize your great aunt's estate himself."

"Of course not," I said. "He's too busy."

"He's too selfish! All that man cares about is himself: his cars, his house, his career, his fame."

I wanted to defend him, but I could see Mom was starting to choke up. She angrily wiped at her eyes and continued. "You don't see your father like I do. You don't see him pouring his life into this family day and night when no one else is looking, when no one else seems to care.

"He's always there for us, Wally. Always. He may not have all the cool things or be superpopular or famous. He may not have the fancy job or look the part of a hero. But your father *is* a hero, Wally. He's more of a hero than your Uncle Max will ever be. He's ten times the hero of your Uncle Max."

With that she rose to her feet and glanced around a little lost. She obviously hadn't planned to get that upset. Then, wiping her eyes, she regained her composure. "Go ahead and get your stuff ready." She started toward the door. "If we're taking you to Fantasmo World, you better get a move on."

Chapter 7

Rehearsal

"Okay everybody, listen up." The stunt coordinator for the show, a big muscular guy with less hair than a hard-boiled egg, got everyone's attention. "Julie's sick, so we have a new cast member." He pointed to where I stood. "Everybody say hi to Molly."

Thirty-five actors in costume turned to me. Some of them were dressed up like marching band members, others like Sasquatches, and others like soldiers.

"Hi, Molly," they shouted.

"Actually it's Wally," I said, pushing up a band hat that was about ten sizes too big.

"Molly, Wally who can tell in that get-up?" The coordinator laughed. Everyone chuckled with him.

By get up, he wasn't only talking about my goofy hat. He was also referring to the rest of my costume. My band uniform was so big that my twin brothers could wear it . . . at the same time.

I pulled up my pants for the hundredth time and looked for Uncle Max. He said he'd be around to help. So far he was nowhere to be seen. I've got to admit it was a little nerve-racking hanging here all by myself with all these strangers.

We stood in a stadium made to look like a town square in Alaska. It had everything—stores, a band stand, a giant totem pole. Directly behind us was what was supposed to be a huge dam, holding back an even huger river. Of course everything was fake, but from the grandstands nobody could tell.

The stunt coordinator continued to give me instructions. "Now the scene goes like this, Molly."

"Wally," I corrected.

"Whatever. You're busy marching in the high school band. A herd of Bigfeet come down from the mountains and invade your town. But it's actually a trap set up by the army that's using you guys as live bait."

I gave my pants another pull.

"Anyway, the army comes out from behind those buildings to save you guys. And of course they start blowing up everything in sight—you know, with rifles, bazookas, missiles—the usual smoke and fire stuff. All the actors run for their lives. Then the king of the Bigfeet—Sid, where are you?"

"Over here." The man I'd met in the tunnel the day before gave me a wave.

"Sid kidnaps you from the band and climbs that totem pole. Of course bazookas and bombs are flying all around. Unfortunately, one of the shells accidentally hits that dam behind you, and it bursts open. Water pours in everywhere. Then one explodes at the base of the totem pole causing the whole thing to tilt."

"Excuse me, excuse me." I was waving my hand faster than a first grader who has to go to the bathroom.

"Yeah, Molly?"

"If there's bazookas and missiles flying, what's going to stop one from hitting us?"

Everyone laughed. I felt like a jerk but figured if I was going to die it would be nice to know a few of the details.

The stunt coordinator answered. "Most are just charges set to explode in the ground. But the rockets and bazookas shoot along tiny wires. As long as you don't stand near the wires, you'll be perfectly safe."

This was obviously a new definition of perfectly safe.

"Just stay with me," Sid called. "Once I grabs ya from the marching band, you'll be with me the whole time."

"Until he drops you in the water," the coordinator said.

"Water?" I croaked. "I'm not the greatest swimmer."

"Don't worry, Wally, I am." I spun around to see Uncle Max coming from behind one of the stores. He flashed that famous smile, and a wave of relief washed over me. Now I knew I'd be safe.

"I'll show up from behind this building on a jet ski," he said. "I'll race up to you, snatch you out of the water, and save the day."

I couldn't help smiling. It sounded great.

He gave me a wink. "Don't worry, kid. You'll do swell."

"All right," the stunt coordinator yelled. "Places, please."

We started rehearsal, and it went fine. Well, the first five seconds went fine. That's when I marched down the street with the other band members. We all pretended to play our instruments to pre-recorded music.

No problem . . . except for the part where I couldn't see out from under my hat. Then, of course, there was the giant tuba I had to carry. It was so heavy that I was doing more staggering than marching. Back and forth and forth and back.

The good news was I did it in step to the music, so I figured nobody would notice.

The bad news was I was wrong.

BUMP.

"Hey, watch it!"
"Sorry."

TROMP.

"Hey, that's my foot."
"Sorry."
And then came the big one.

K-SMAAASHSH!

"Look out! Molly just crashed into the totem pole! Look out everybody, it's coming down! *Timber!*"

CRASH! CRUNCH . . .
Tinkle, tinkle, tinkle.

"Stop the music!" the coordinator shouted. "Stop the music!"

We all came to a stop. I pushed up my hat. That was about when I noticed the marching band was on the opposite side of the stadium from me. Then, of course, there was the totem pole . .. the one I'd just knocked over . . . the one that had just fallen into the entire row of store windows, smashing out all of their glass. (Now you know what the *tinkle, tinkle, tinkle* was all about.)

Everyone slowly turned from the stores to the totem pole to me. By their looks of amazement, I could tell they'd never been exposed to such incredible clumsiness.

"Well," the coordinator took a deep breath and sighed. "That was quite a performance, Molly. But not quite the one I had in mind." He turned to a crew member who was already examining my handiwork. "How long will it take to fix the totem pole and those windows?"

"Looks like a couple of hours, boss. But we'll have to clear the area."

"All right," the coordinator shouted to the cast. "That'll have to do. We'll see you all at 2:00 for the show."

Everybody nodded and started to leave.

"But . . ." I searched the crowd for Uncle Max. Unfortunately, he had already disappeared.

"But, but . . ." Finally I saw Sid and ran up to him. "But, but, but . . ."

"Spit it out, kid."

"I don't know what to do."

"You'll have to fake it," he said.

"But . . ."

"Just stay with me. I'll carry ya through it."

He patted me on the head and walked off.

I tried to smile, but, I definitely had some big time doubts. I mean, if I did that badly in the rehearsal, I could only imagine what could go wrong in the show.

Unfortunately, even my imagination wouldn't be good enough for this one.

* * * * *

We had a some time to kill before the show. And since Uncle Max was still in the midst of his vanishing routine, I decided to hang out with Sid. We entered the tunnel and stayed in a special room where the cast members waited before the show.

Because I was kind of nervous and a lot scared, I did what I always do when I'm nervous and scared. I tried to take my mind off it by writing. I whipped out ol' Betsy and started to work on my Floss Man story.

When we last left Floss Man, he'd just fluttered down a smokestack. Now he is leaping out into the notorious and not so nice hideout of (more bad guy music, please)... Harry the Haircube.

But he barely steps into the room

before he comes to a stop. There are soap bubbles everywhere. Not the cool, round kind. Instead these have sharper and pointier edges than a punker's haircut. Some are perfect cubes; others are rectangles. A few pyramids even float by. And each and every one is filled with a sinister smoke.

Our hero tries to look past them, but there are so many he can't even see across the room.

"Wh□...*c□ugh c□ugh, hack hack*...are y□u?" a voice shouts from the other end of the building.

"I'm Floss Man, and I've come to stop your diabolical deeds...and to make sure you brush after every meal."

"T□□ late," Haircube laughs. "Each □f these bubbles is filled with a t□xic ...*hack hack, c□ugh c□ugh*...gas that makes all curves int□ c□rners. I'm fl□ating them int□ the w□rld where they will p□p and release their terrible t□xicness."

"But why?" Floss Man cries, doing his best to dodge the floating bubbles.

"Why n□t?"

Floss Man scrunches up his forehead, trying to find an answer. But such logic is too powerful for our hero (what do you expect from a piece of string?). So, before he completely sprains his brain, Floss Man quickly moves to Plan B (which is a lot like Plan A except for where it's different).

He races through the room, dodging each and every bubble. Sometimes there's only a thread's width between the slippery soapsters, but that's all he needs. (What strings lack in smarts they make up for in skinniness).

"What...*c□ugh hack, c□ugh hack*...are y□u d□ing!" Haircube cries.

"I've got to make you see reason," our hero shouts as he expertly slips between the bubbles.

"Stay...*hack c□ugh*...back!"

But Floss Man will not give up. (It's in the fine print of his superhero contract, right along with not smoking, chewing tobacco, or kissing girls who do.) He pushes forward. Soon he spots the hacking Haircube. The foul furriness is standing beside an even fouler bubble machine. It's filling each and every bubble with gas from the even foulerer ...Toxic Gas Makerer.

But Floss Man will not be put off by

such bad spelling. Before Haircube knows what has hit him, Floss Man leaps at him and quickly wraps himself around the bad guy's feet.

"St□p it! *c□ugh* St□p it! *hack*"

But his protests do little good. Soon, the phlegm-filled fiend loses his balance and topples to the ground.

Quickly, Floss Man wraps himself around the Haircube's arms and hands (good thing our hero comes in the large, econo size). Expertly, he ties him up in granny knots, slipknots, and—but wait! Every one of those knots has curves.

Uh-oh.

Immediately, Haircube bangs his head into one of the nearby bubbles. It pops and releases its toxic gas on Floss Man's handiwork. The tightly tied knots suddenly loosen and the square corners give Haircube plenty of room to slip free.

"All right, String Thing," he sneers as he leaps to his feet. "Y□u want t□ play r□ugh...*c□ugh c□ugh, spit spit*...(oh no, now he's really getting gross) we'll play r□ugh."

Before Floss Man can defend himself,

Haircube grabs one end of our hero's flimsy frame and flings the fine fellow flying. (Say that with a mouthful of crackers.) Then, effortlessly, the bad guy with the even badder bronchitis points his bubble machine directly at Floss Man. He pulls the trigger. Immediately a giant bubble flies out, wraps around our hero, and imprisons him.

"Har har...*hack hack...more spitting, more spitting*...Let's see y□u get □ut □f this, y□u tirelessly tr□ublesome thread."

Oh no, how will Floss Man ever get free? How will he survive? And most important, how will he ever get under Haircube's gums to get rid of the plaque that brushing just can't reach? Before these and other unimportant questions can be answered, he suddenly—

"Okay, Molly."

I looked up. The stunt coordinator smiled down on me.

"It's showtime."

Chapter 8

It's Showtime, Folks

"All right, roll tape," the stunt coordinator shouted into his headset.

Marching music blasted through the stadium speakers, and everyone in our little band got into step. Well, everyone in our little band but me. I was still busy tripping over my elephant-sized uniform, staggering under the weight of my tuba, and trying to see out from under my hat. Fortunately, they put me in the center of the band, so I was trapped. I couldn't stray too far without bumping into someone.

"And . . . ACTION!" the coordinator shouted.

We started forward, marched around the corner, and entered the stadium. It was filled with a gazillion people all sitting in the stands, staring at us eagerly.

It was awesome.

We marched toward the town square, pretending

to play our instruments. Of course I was busy doing my human pinball imitation, bouncing off the other band members, but I figured that was okay. At least this way my family could tell where I was.

"There's Wally!" I imagined Carrie pointing and crying out from the stands.

"How can you tell?" Mom would shout in excitement.

"Who else would be that klutzy?" Burt and Brock would yawn in bored unison.

The band had nearly come to the totem pole when we heard incredibly loud shrieking and screaming.

We stopped.

"Oh . . . no, what . . . is . . . that?" one of the actors beside me shouted.

"Oh . . . my, it . . . is . . . a . . . herd . . . of . . . attacking . . . Bigfeet," another actor cried.

"Oh . . . dear, I . . . guess . . . we . . . had . . . better . . . run."

"Oh . . . yes, I . . . guess . . . you . . . are . . . right."

After that stupendous display of acting, the band members screamed, dropped their instruments, and raced out of the stadium.

Well, all of the band members but me. Since we'd never gotten this far in rehearsal, I wasn't sure what to do. I figured now would be as good a time as any to push up my hat to take a look.

I wished I hadn't.

About a dozen Bigfeet were racing into town from my left. That wasn't the problem, I knew they were just actors. The problem was all the arrows and flaming spears they were throwing . . . in my direction!

ZIP, ZIP, ZIP . . .
SINGE.

YEOW! That last one was just a little too close. It managed to ignite the dorky little feather on my band hat.

Desperately I looked around for Sid. He was supposed to come in and scoop me up. Unfortunately, it was about this time that I noticed about a hundred army guys (complete with blazing bazookas, missiles, and a tank) coming in from my right.

WHOOSH, WHOOSH, WHOOSH . . .

Great, I was trapped in a crossfire. The Bigfeet stormed in from my left with their flaming arrows

ZIP, ZIP, ZIP . . .

And the army came at me from the right with their missiles and bazookas.

WHOOSH, WHOOSH, WHOOSH . . .

I was surrounded.

K-BOOM! K-BOOM! K-BOOM!

Wonderful, now all those army missiles and bazookas were exploding around my feet.

What to do?

ZIP, ZIP, ZIP . . .

There was no place to run.

WHOOSH, WHOOSH, WHOOSH . . .

No place to hide.

K-BOOM! K-BOOM! K-BOOM!

Well, almost no place . . .

I still had my tuba. And being the part-time genius (and full-time coward) that I am, I quickly set the tuba down and squirmed inside the giant instrument until my head and chest were safely protected. So there I was, doing my best ostrich imitation, being safe and perfectly sound in my new tuba.

ZIP-DING, ZIP-DING,
ZIP-DING . . .

Nice try boys, but there's no way you can penetrate my armored tuba.

WHOOSH-DING, WHOOSH-DING,
WHOOSH-DING . . .

And I was right. Well, except for one minor little detail.

RUMBLE, RUMBLE, RUMBLE . . .

What was that?!

RUMBLE, RUMBLE,
RUMBLE . . .

Whatever it was, it was getting louder, and fast. I adjusted myself inside the tuba until I could see out one of the spit valves.

RUMBLE, RUMBLE,
RUMBLE . . .

It was a tank! A real, honest to goodness Army tank. And, as McDoogle luck would have it, it was heading straight for me!

I wasn't sure where Sid was. And I wasn't sure why Uncle Max hadn't leaped out and stopped the show. But since neither seemed to be around and since the tank was getting closer by the second, I did the only thing I could do.

I struggled to my feet and started to run.

ZIP-DING, ZIP-DING, ZIP-DING . . .

Of course the tuba was still over my head, which caused more than a few people to laugh. (When was the last time you saw a running tuba?)

WHOOSH-DING, WHOOSH-DING,
WHOOSH-DING . . .

I had no idea where I was going, but at least I was protected. At least I was safe inside my—

KLUNK-THUD.

Well, I had been safe. Unfortunately the KLUNK was me bouncing off the front end of the tank. And the THUD was me falling to the ground.

But this didn't bother me as much as the next sound.

CRUNCH, CRUNCH, CRUNCH, CRUNCH . . .

Obviously, my tuba got caught up in the tank treads. Even that wasn't so bad, compared to the very last sound I heard.

"AUGH . . . HHH . . . HHH . . ."

My screams echoed in my tuba as I started going round and round with the tank treads.

And then, just when things couldn't get any worse (and I couldn't get any dizzier) I suddenly felt myself hoisted high into the air.

I figured now would be a good time to scream even louder. Until suddenly I tumbled out of the tuba and into the arms of a giant Bigfoot.

"Sid, is that you?" I cried.

"Of course!" The voice came out muffled through the costume head he was wearing.

WHOOSH, WHOOSH, WHOOSH . . .

"Those army guys," I cried, "they're shooting real bazookas."

"Nah. The rockets are following the tracer wire, remember? They're exploding where they're connected to the ground."

"But they've been hitting me!"

"That's 'cause you've been standing in the center of the wires."

"Oh." It figured. If there was some place unsafe to stand, I had to be the one standing there.

"Now this is the tricky part," he shouted through his costume head. "Just do a lot of yelling while I start to climb up this totem pole. Oh, and try to look scared."

No problem there.

With that he threw me over his shoulder and started climbing the pole.

Meanwhile, our army buddies were still pretending to shoot. Suddenly the fake dam behind us exploded.

"Oh . . . no!" one of the army guys shouted, his acting even worse than the band members' had been. "One . . . of . . . my . . . rockets . . . has . . . hit . . . the . . . dam. Dear . . . me, now . . . I . . . have . . . gone . . . and . . . done . . . it!"

Fortunately, you could barely hear his bad acting over the thundering of the water as it roared out of the fake hole in the fake dam. The only problem was it pounded and roared directly toward us!

"Sid!" I shouted, "the dam is—"

"It's all fake!" he shouted over the roar. "Just giant water pipes shooting water through that hole and flooding the stadium."

I watched as the water raged and pounded

under us. Somehow I suspected a person could drown just as easily in a fake flood as in a real one.

I looked toward the building Uncle Max was supposed to jet ski around for his grand entrance. A bunch of jet skis were parked there, but he was nowhere in sight. And for good reason. The two thugs that had dropped by for breakfast, the ones he owed money to, were there instead.

Uh-oh.

And they were looking all over for him.

Double uh-oh.

"Okay, get ready!" Sid shouted through his costume.

"Yeah, but—"

"I'm going to raise ya to my mouth like I'm going to eat ya. That's the cue for the army guys to fire a bazooka and hit the totem pole."

"Yeah, but—"

"Then I'll drop ya into the water and your Uncle Max will come save ya."

"Yeah, but—"

Before I could explain that Uncle Max wasn't around to save my life, Sid let out a growl. "ARRRGHHHHHHH!"

I'll have to say it was pretty convincing. But, before I could compliment him on his acting ability, he raised me high into the air and opened his mouth.

Of course the audience was going crazy. People took pictures left and right as he held me up, preparing to chomp into me. It was a great photo opportunity but I was kind of sad realizing these last few seconds on earth would immortalize me forever simply a Bigfoot breath mint.

And then it happened.

K-BOOOOOOOOOM!

The totem pole shuddered under the explosion and Sid released me, just as we planned. Well, just as he planned.

"AUGGHHHHHH . . ." I screamed as I fell into the thundering water.

The current was strong and the water swirled and raged. It was all I could do to fight my way back up to the surface to get a breath of air. Desperately, I looked for Uncle Max, but he was nowhere to be seen.

Then the current dragged me back down under the water.

Chapter 9

Unlikely Hero

Don't get me wrong, I like a good swim as much as the next guy. I just have this thing about breathing. And the way the water was pulling me under and throwing me all around, it didn't look like I'd be getting the chance to do that for a while.

Beneath the surface, everything was swirling water and bubbles. I didn't know which way was up. Finally I caught a glimpse of distant light. I kicked off my shoes and swam toward it. Then I surfaced with more than the daily minimum requirement of coughing and choking.

"Uncle Max!" I shouted. "Where's Uncle—"

And then I heard it. The roar of a jet ski. I spun around and broke into a grin. There he was, heading toward me. What a relief. It was still rough keeping my head above the water, but at least I knew I was about to be saved.

Then I noticed it. The closer he came, the more

it looked like he wasn't heading for me after all. In fact it looked like he was going to go right past me!

I waved my arms. "Uncle *choke* Max! I'm *cough cough* over here!"

He caught a glimpse of me out of the corner of his eye and changed course. Now he was heading directly toward me. Good, that was better. A lot better.

He started to slow down and leaned over, getting ready to scoop me up.

"I knew you'd come!" I coughed.

He forced a smile then glanced nervously over his shoulder. When he turned back I saw his expression had completely changed. Without a warning, he suddenly gunned his jet ski . . . and roared right past me.

"UNCLE MAX! UNCLE—"

My cries did no good. He didn't even look back as he raced for the other side of the stadium.

"UNCLE—*choke choke, glug glug* . . ."

The wake of his jet ski pulled me under the water.

When I came back up, he was still making his getaway and disappearing rapidly. What was happening? Why had he deserted me? I was clueless. I had no idea what was going on (other than the minor fact that I was still drowning to death).

Then I heard another sound. I spun around and had my answer.

The two thugs were also on jet skis and quickly closing in.

I did my usual shouting and screaming for help, but for some reason they had other things on their minds. They raced right by me without so much as a snarl. They did, however, leave giant wakes behind, which sent me back under the water again.

Yes sir, it was just like old times, spinning and turning in the bubbling water. I swam for all I was worth (which was getting to be less and less), but this time I didn't see daylight.

I swam harder.

Still nothing.

I began to panic. My lungs started to burn for air. And still no light. About this time I came to an incredible conclusion. Either someone had unplugged the sun, or I was swimming in the wrong direction.

I spun around and kicked off the other way.

And then I saw it. A faint light, but it was far, far away. I swam harder. My lungs were on fire, screaming for air. The light looked closer, but I doubted I could make it. Still I swam, my lungs ready to explode. My mind raced with thoughts of who'd get my CD player and, more important, would I have to spend eternity in heaven wearing this lame band uniform?

Then, somehow, some way I surfaced. I did more coughing and choking than the Haircube character in my superhero story. I'd never drowned before, and I have to admit I really didn't want to learn now. But I didn't have enough strength to make it back to shore. I knew I couldn't survive another dunk. It would only be a matter of seconds before—

Then I heard it.

"Hang on, Wally . . ."

The voice was distant but grew louder.

"Hang on, Wally. I'm coming."

It was Dad!

I spun around and caught a glimpse of his balding head bobbing through the waves toward me. What's he doing?! He can't swim! He's scared to death of the water!

But yet he just kept on coming.

"Hang on, son!"

Another wave hit. I fought to stay on the surface, but my arms and legs were giving out.

"Hang on . . ."

Behind the wave came a major swirl. It caught me and dragged me back under for what I knew was the last time.

I couldn't hold on. I was giving in, giving up. I

didn't want to swim anymore. I couldn't. I had nothing to swim with. Suddenly dying didn't seem like such a bad deal after all. (Although it could definitely put a crimp in your summer vacation plans.) All I had to do was stop fighting, just give up. All I had to do was take a deep breath of water and it would all be over. The fire in my lungs would go out, and I'd just keep on sinking . . . forever. Floating . . . sinking . . .

Suddenly, I felt an arm wrap around my chest. It was pulling on me—hard.

A moment later I was yanked to the surface, doing what I do best: coughing and gagging my insides out. But this time I had company. This time Dad was right beside me coughing and choking even more than I was.

"What are you doing out here?" I shouted. "You can't swim!"

"Tell me about it," he coughed. "I don't know the first thing about—"

Another big wave hit us and we both went under. But instead of giving up and letting go, I wanted to fight. I wasn't sure why or how, but something about having Dad out there, something about his caring, gave me strength. And with that strength I fought and kicked my way back to the surface.

I came up coughing but couldn't see Dad.

"Dad? DAD?!"

He was still under the water!

I dove back in. It was hard to see through the murky water and bubbles, but at last I found him. He was thrashing wildly in all directions at the same time . . . which meant he was getting nowhere fast. I grabbed his sleeve and pulled and kicked us both toward the surface.

At last we made it to air and continued our choking and coughing routine.

"You can't swim worth beans!" I shouted.

"You're wrong," Dad half laughed, half choked. "I can't swim at all!"

Strange, here we were getting ready to die, and we were busy cracking jokes.

"Take off your coat!" I shouted. "And your shoes. You've still got your shoes on!"

"I was in kind of a hurry!"

Another wave washed over us, and we were dunked back under. But only for a second.

When we came back up, Dad shouted, "Let me grab you around the chest."

"What?!"

"I've seen it on TV," he shouted. "It's how lifeguards save people."

I shook my head. "I'm the swimmer, let me save you!"

"You don't have the strength!"

"You don't know how to swim!"

Another wave, another dunk.

When we came back up, Dad had a solution. "All right, let's take turns."

"What?"

"You swim us toward shore a few strokes. When you get tired, rest and I'll try to keep us floating until you regain your strength!"

I looked at him. I wanted to tell him he was crazy, but something in his eyes stopped me. I can't exactly explain it, but there was something in them that I had never seen before. Maybe it had always been there. Maybe I'd just never noticed it. I don't know. But I do know his eyes were filled with such love for me that I felt a lump grow in my throat.

It wasn't a great plan, but it seemed to be the only one we had. I nodded and shouted, "Okay, let's give it a shot."

And so we started for shore. Me hanging onto Dad, and Dad hanging onto me. I'd take my five or six strokes before having to rest, then Dad would do his best to keep our heads above water. Then I'd take another five or six strokes and rest again.

It was slow going, and we were definitely taking in more than our recommended eight glasses of water per day. But gradually, foot by foot, we made progress.

Yes sir, we were quite the team, though I wouldn't be looking for us at the Olympics. Eventually, I could see the grandstands. We were much closer. And then, for some strange reason, we started picking up speed. My swimming became easier and easier.

"We're in some sort of current," I shouted.

"That's great!" Dad yelled.

But it wasn't great. At first we had been pushed toward the grandstands, but now we were being pulled away. Then we were pushed back again, faster this time. And then pulled away, even faster.

"We're in a whirlpool!" Dad shouted.

"A what?!"

"The stadium is draining! We're being sucked down into a drain!"

I looked around. Dad was right. We were entering a giant cone of water. We were spinning around, faster and faster, in tighter and tighter circles. It was almost as bad as that twister movie . . . but without the popcorn and Coke!

And without the air!

The faster we spun, the more the water splashed and covered us.

"I can't fight it!" I cried through the spraying water. "It's too strong!"

"Hang on, son!"

I looked up. We were halfway down the cone. A

wall of water towered high over our heads as the suction continued to drag us down farther and farther. I clung to Dad for all I was worth. And he clung to me. I have to admit it had been a long time since we'd hugged each other so tightly. It felt kind of good . . . considering the circumstances.

And then it happened. The cone of water above us caved in. The wall crashed down, slamming tons of water on top of us. I'd like to give you the play-by-play. Unfortunately, it's kind of hard to remember all the details of dying when you've been knocked totally unconscious.

Chapter 10

Wrapping Up

The next thing I remember I was coughing up a swimming pool of water. When I finally opened my eyes, I saw the stunt coordinator hovering over my face. He'd obviously just given me mouth to mouth.

I coughed and sputtered some more.

He turned to the crowd surrounding us. "He's going to be okay, folks."

The faces looking down on me all nodded in approval.

"You all right, sport?"

I looked up and saw Mom kneeling beside me. "Yeah, I think so." I struggled to sit up. "What happened?" Then panic hit me. "What about Dad? Where's—"

"Right here, son."

I turned around and saw Dad sitting on the concrete beside me. He looked pretty wet and wiped out.

"What happened?" I asked. "How did we—" But then, just for old time's sake, I went into a major coughing fit. When I finished, I looked back at Dad. "How did you get us out?"

He brushed what little hair he has out of his eyes and smiled. "I prayed."

"You what?"

He shrugged. "It seemed the right thing to do at the time."

I continued to stare at him. Of course. How could I have forgotten something like that? I mean, there we were, right in the middle of dying, getting ready to make a personal appearance before God. And I hadn't even bothered to ask for His help.

"How?" I croaked. "What happened?"

"It was the most amazing thing," Mom said. "You and Dad were caught in that whirlpool. The two of you really looked like goners."

"We felt like it too," I added.

"And then, at the very last second, your tuba was sucked down into the drain. It completely stopped it up."

"My tuba?" I asked.

"Exactly." Mom grinned. "All the water came crashing together, and it formed this giant wave that shoved you two right up here to the shore. It was a miracle, Wally, a real miracle."

I slowly turned to Dad. I couldn't believe it. But

it wasn't only the miracle that amazed me. Dad did too. I mean, here's this little, no-nothing, balding guy. Not some big superstar. Not some major stunt man. Just plain old Dad. He not only faced his worst fears to try and save my life, but he also had the smarts *and the faith* to pray.

Then I remembered what Mom had said earlier that morning. Maybe she was right. Maybe Uncle Max wasn't such a hero after all. Maybe there was another type of hero in my life, one I had ignored all these years.

The thought made my throat get kind of tight again. Good ol' Dad. Good ol' take-him-for-granted, not-much-into-hugging, always-on-your-case-to-mow-the-lawn Dad. I started to open my mouth. I wanted to say something, to at least thank him, but we were interrupted.

"Step aside. Let me through. I'm the boy's uncle. Let me in." The crowd parted and Uncle Max arrived. "You all right, Wally?"

"What happened?" I asked. "Where did you go?"

"Sorry about that." He flashed his perfect white teeth in his famous ultracool grin. "Remember those guys at breakfast?"

I nodded.

"Well, they had a little unfinished business they wanted to settle with me."

My mouth dropped open. I couldn't believe what

I was hearing. He'd put my life in danger. He'd practically let me drown. And for what? "A little unfinished business?"

Seeing my expression, Uncle Max cranked up his grin to a 10+. "But hey," he slapped me on the back, "everything worked out, didn't it? You got your big break in show biz. You got to star with your Uncle Max in the big stunt extravaganza. You got to . . ."

He continued talking, but I stopped listening. Why hadn't I seen it before? This guy was nothing but show. Oh sure, he could bench press a gazillion pounds, and he had the coolest clothes and house and job. But when the chips were down . . .

I threw a look over to Dad, then back to my uncle. And then, for the very first time, I saw it: the emptiness of Uncle Max's life. I saw his selfishness and shallowness.

For the briefest second his smile drooped. It was almost like he could see what I was thinking. He knew I finally saw how hollow he really was. Once you got past all his flash, there was . . . well, there was nothing.

"Excuse me, excuse us please." A couple of guys with a video camera and microphone were shoving their way through the crowd. "Excuse us. Is this the kid?" they asked, pointing at me and pushing in closer. "Are you Molly McDoogle?"

"Uh, no," Uncle Max said, cranking his smile back up to its megabrightness. He tousled my hair, "This is *Wally* McDoogle. And I'm his Uncle Max."

"Great," they said, turning on their camera and shoving a microphone into his face. "So you're the boy's uncle, the stunt man who saved his life."

Uncle Max chuckled. "Well, I wouldn't go that far . . . though I am the featured star in this stunt show."

The rest was kind of a blur. Though I remember being amazed at how Uncle Max took every question and kind of turned it on himself. Of course I tried to explain what actually happened, but it didn't seem to do any good. The reporter already had his story: "Stunt Man Saves Nephew." And there didn't seem to be anything I could do to change it.

I remember looking over at Dad, who was now standing with the rest of the crowd watching. He wasn't mad. In fact he just stood there kind of beaming at me. Funny. The guy was so proud that I would be on the evening news. It didn't even dawn on him that he should step in and take some of the glory for himself.

But it really wasn't that odd. After all, that's the

kind of stuff Dad has been doing for me and my sister and brothers all our lives.

* * * * *

The next morning our suitcases were packed, and we began the journey home. Uncle Max said he couldn't take us to the airport because he had to film another dangerous stunt for Arnold Swizzlenoggin. So he hired a fancy stretch limo to take us there instead.

Of course everyone was all hugs, kisses, and "come back again real soon"s. But I could tell Uncle Max couldn't wait for us to get out of his hair. The reason was pretty clear. . . . Some of us had finally figured out who he really was.

Riding inside the limo was pretty cool. But you can only play with the TV remote or the CD player or open the refrigerator and spill Diet Dr. Pepper all over yourself so many times before you get a little bored.

So, after wringing out my clothes, I reached down for ol' Betsy, turned her on, and checked out how Floss Man and Haircube were doing.

When we last left our anorexically thin thread, he was inside a giant soap

bubble, floating up, up, and away. No doubt, being the intelligent reader you are (hey, you figured out what anorexically meant, didn't you?—or did you just fake it and move on?). Anyway, you're probably wondering why our hero didn't just pop the bubble with his finger and get out. But fingers require hands, which require arms, which are a bit on the rare side for dental floss.

So now Floss Man is standing inside the bubble, desperately trying to think of some way out. But since brains are even rarer than hands for him, the thinking does him little good. Sadly, he plops down. But as luck would have it, the comb in his back pocket sticks through the bubble and bursts it.

Gently he flutters back to earth. But instead of joining the horrendously hateful and hacking Haircube, he lands atop the giant Toxic Gas Maker.

As he tries to climb down, our long, stringy hero accidentally gets himself tangled in all the wheels and gears and stuff. (Talk about being tied up in knots.) In a matter of seconds, the giant machine is so bound up that it begins to groan and moan under the strain.

"What are you d□ing?" Haircube cries. "What are you *hack hack* d□ing?"

At last the Toxic Gas Maker grinds to a halt. The ghastly gas is no longer gassing.

"Unfair!" Haircube screams. "Unfair!"

"*Au contraire,*" Floss Man answers. (That's French for "on the contrary" in case you have to write a book report telling what you've learned from this masterpiece.) "It is you who is unfair."

"What d□ you *c□ugh c□ugh* mean?"

"Not everyone likes corners as much as you do. Who are you to tell people that they can't have round?"

"I'm the bad guy, remember?"

"Oh yeah." (More dental floss genius.) He tries another angle. "But, tell me, why did you do this dastardly deed in the first place?"

"Why?" Haircube cries, "I'll tell y□u why. All □f my life I wanted t□ be s□meb□dy. I wanted t□ be n□ticed. I wanted t□ be a her□."

"And you thought ridding the planet of everything round would do it?"

"It sure beats raising pet r□cks."

"But you don't have to be noticed and famous to be a hero."

"I d□n't?"

"No way. Look at me. I'm just a flimsy piece of waxed string. All I do is quietly clean people's teeth and make their lives a little bit better."

"Except when y□u make their gums bleed."

Floss Man nods but will not be dissuaded (oh, another cool word to look up) from continuing his wrap up. "You don't have to be famous or special to be a hero. You can be a hero by just quietly helping other people."

"Y□u mean by helping cats and d□gs."

"Pardon me?"

"Hairballs d□n't help pe□ple. We're m□re □f a cats and d□gs thing."

"I see. Well, the point is, heroes are really just people who go about quietly helping others."

"But I'll never get t□ star in the m□vies that way," Haircube complains.

"True, but you'll touch people's lives in ways they will never forget."

"W□w," Haircube exclaims as he hears

the wrap-up music start to play, "that w□uld be just nifty c□□l. S□ tell me, h□w can I be this quiet her□ y□u're talking ab□ut?"

"Let's begin by reversing the effects of this toxic gas and making things round again, shall we?"

"What a super swell idea."

"What?" Floss Man shouts over the music (which is even cornier than this ending).

"Never mind," Haircube calls, "let's get started bef□re they start r□lling credits."

And so, having learned his lesson, Harry the Hairball joins Floss Man in rebuilding the Toxic Gas Maker to reverse its effects. Soon the world will be a safer place for frisbees, wheels, and basketball stars, who have been losing their minds trying to dribble basketcubes.

I stared at the screen. It was definitely a three cavity ending. (Translation: It was so sweet it made my teeth hurt.) But, thanks to Dad, I was feeling a bit on the sentimental side, so it was okay. I reached over and shut ol' Betsy down just as we pulled up to the curb at the airport terminal.

Yes sir, visiting Los Angeles had been quite an eye-opener. Not only did it help me see what was real, but it also helped me understand what was important. Oh sure, it would be cool to have a famous dad, with the big bucks, fancy cars, and an ultracool lifestyle. But I had something even more valuable. I had a dad who cared. Maybe he's not a flashy, look-at-me kind of guy. But he's someone who, every day, gives up just a little bit of his life so that mine can be just a little bit better.

As I was stepping out of the limo, Burt began to shout from inside. "Hey, check it out. Everybody!"

I stuck my head back into the car just in time to see the interview they had taped of Uncle Max and me. Well, the interview they had taped of Uncle Max. Somehow they had managed to edit most of me out.

"They got Uncle Max on the news," Burt shouted. "They're making him out to be a real hero."

Carrie and Brock scrambled back inside to watch, but I decided to go around and help Mom and Dad unload the trunk.

"What's the matter?" Dad asked as I joined him.

"Don't you want to see your Uncle Max on the news?"

"Nah," I said, struggling to pull a suitcase twice my size out of the trunk. "I already know what he looks like."

Dad said nothing.

"Besides," I turned to him and grinned, "I know who the real heroes are."

Dad stopped and looked at me, kind of puzzled. He obviously didn't get it. But that was okay. I did. And from the grin on Mom's face, I knew she did too.

I pulled out the suitcase and immediately began to stagger under its weight.

"Oooo . . ."

"Ahhh . . ."

"Eeee . . ."

SCREECH . . .

CRASH! CRASH! CRASH! CRASH!

The *Oooos, Ahhhs*, and *Eeees* were me stumbling out onto the road under the weight of the suitcase.

The *SCREECH* was a car slamming on its brakes, trying not to turn me into road kill.

And the *CRASH*es were that car's rear end being slammed into by another, which was slammed into by another, which was . . . well, I'm sure you get the picture.

"Wally . . ."

I turned to see Dad groaning and shaking his head.

Yes sir, it was great to be heading back home. It was even better to know that things were already starting to get back to normal.

About the Author

Bill Myers is the author and co-creator of the best-selling "McGee and Me!" book and video series, which has sold more than 2 million episodes and has appeared several times as ABC's Weekend Special. He has written more than three dozen books, including the children's series "Journeys to Fayrah" and "Forbidden Doors," as well as the best-selling adult novel "Blood of Heaven." His work as a film maker has earned more than 40 national and international awards. When he's not roaming the world making movies, he enjoys speaking at conferences and working with the youth of his local church. Bill lives in California with his wife, Brenda, and their two children.

You'll want to read them all.

THE INCREDIBLE WORLDS OF WALLY McDOOGLE

#1—My Life As a Smashed Burrito with Extra Hot Sauce

Twelve-year-old Wally—"The walking disaster area"—is forced to stand up to Camp Wahkah Wahkah's number one all-American bad guy. One hilarious mishap follows another until, fighting together for their very lives, Wally learns the need for even his worst enemy to receive Jesus Christ. (ISBN 0–8499–3402–8)

#2—My Life As Alien Monster Bait

"Hollyweird" comes to Middletown! Wally's a superstar! A movie company has chosen our hero to be eaten by their mechanical "Mutant from Mars!" It's a close race as to which will consume Wally first—the disaster-plagued special effects "monster" or his own out-of-control pride . . . until he learns the cost of true friendship and of God's command for humility. (ISBN 0–8499–3403–6)

#3—My Life As a Broken Bungee Cord

A hot-air balloon race! What could be more fun? Then again, we're talking about Wally McDoogle, the "Human Catastrophe." Calamity builds on calamity until, with his life on the line, Wally learns what it means to FULLY put his trust in God. (ISBN 0–8499–3404–4)

#4—My Life As Crocodile Junk Food

Wally visits missionary friends in the South American rain forest. Here he stumbles onto a whole new set of impossible predicaments . . . until he understands the need and joy of sharing Jesus Christ with others.
(ISBN 0–8499–3405–2)

#5—My Life As Dinosaur Dental Floss

It starts with a practical joke that snowballs into near disaster. Risking his life to protect his country, Wally is pursued by a SWAT team, bungling terrorists, photo-snapping tourists, Gary the Gorilla, and a TV news reporter. After prehistoric-size mishaps and a talk with the President, Wally learns that maybe honesty really is the best policy. (ISBN 0–8499–3537–7)

#6—My Life As a Torpedo Test Target

Wally uncovers the mysterious secrets of a sunken submarine. As dreams of fame and glory increase, so do the famous McDoogle mishaps. Besides hostile sea creatures, hostile pirates, and hostile Wally McDoogle clumsiness, there is the war against his own greed and selfishness. It isn't until Wally finds himself on a wild ride atop a misguided torpedo that he realizes the source of true greatness. (ISBN 0–8499–3538–5)

#7—My Life As a Human Hockey Puck

Look out . . . Wally McDoogle turns athlete! Jealousy and envy drive Wally from one hilarious calamity to another until, as the team's mascot, he learns humility while suddenly being thrown in to play goalie for the Middletown Super Chickens! (ISBN 0–8499–3601–2)

#8—My Life As an Afterthought Astronaut

"Just cause I didn't follow the rules doesn't make it my fault that the Space Shuttle almost crashed. Well, okay, maybe it was sort of my fault. But not the part when Pilot O'Brien was spacewalking and I accidently knocked him halfway to Jupiter. . . ." So begins another hilarious Wally McDoogle MISadventure as our boy blunder stows aboard the Space Shuttle and learns the importance of: Obeying the Rules!
(ISBN 0–8499–3602–0)

#9—My Life As Reindeer Road Kill

Santa on an out-of-control four wheeler? Electrical Rudolph on the rampage? Nothing unusual, just Wally McDoogle doing some last-minute Christmas shopping . . . FOR GOD! Our boy blunder dreams that an angel has invited him to a birthday party for Jesus. Chaos and comedy follow as he turns the town upside down looking for the perfect gift, until he finally bumbles his way into the real reason for the Season. (ISBN 0–8499–3866–x)

#10—My Life As a Toasted Time Traveler

Wally travels back from the future to warn himself of an upcoming accident. But before he knows it, there are more Wallys running around than even Wally himself can handle. Catastrophes reach an all-time high as Wally tries to out-think God and re-write history. (ISBN 0–8499–3867–8)

#11—My Life As Polluted Pond Scum

This laugh-filled McDoogle disaster includes: a monster lurking in the depths of a mysterious lake . . . a glowing figure with powers to summon the creature to the shore . . . and one Wally McDoogle, who reluctantly stumbles upon the truth. Wally's entire town is in danger. And he must race against the clock, his own fears, and his world renown Klutziness—and learn to trust God—before he has any chance of saving the day. (ISBN 0–8499–3875–9)